PUFFIN BOOKS

Sheltie Gallops Ahead

Make friends with

The little pony with the big heart

Sheltie is the lovable little Shetland pony with a big personality. His best friend and owner is Emma, and together they have lots of exciting adventures.

Share Sheltie and Emma's adventures in

SHELTIE THE SHETLAND PONY
SHELTIE SAVES THE DAY
SHELTIE AND THE RUNAWAY
SHELTIE FINDS A FRIEND
SHELTIE TO THE RESCUE
SHELTIE IN DANGER
SHELTIE RIDES TO WIN
SHEL̶̶̶̶̶̶̶̶STERY

S̶̶̶̶̶̶̶̶ONY
SHELTIE ON PARADE
SHELTIE FOR EVER
SHELTIE ON PATROL

Peter Clover was born and went to school in London. He was a storyboard artist and illustrator before he began to put words to his pictures. He enjoys painting, travelling, cooking and keeping fit, and lives on the coast in Somerset.

Also by Peter Clover in Puffin

The Sheltie series

Sheltie
Gallops Ahead

Peter Clover

PUFFIN BOOKS

For John, Steven and Alice

PUFFIN BOOKS

Published by the Penguin Group
Penguin Books Ltd, 27 Wrights Lane, London W8 5TZ, England
Penguin Putnam Inc., 375 Hudson Street, New York, New York 10014, USA
Penguin Books Australia Ltd, Ringwood, Victoria, Australia
Penguin Books Canada Ltd, 10 Alcorn Avenue, Toronto, Ontario, Canada M4V 3B2
Penguin Books (NZ) Ltd, Private Bag 102902, NSMC, Auckland, New Zealand

On the World Wide Web at: www.penguin.com

Penguin Books Ltd, Registered Offices: Harmondsworth, Middlesex, England

First published 1999
1 3 5 7 9 10 8 6 4 2

Sheltie is a trade mark owned by Working Partners Ltd
Copyright © Working Partners Ltd, 1999
All rights reserved

Created by Working Partners Ltd, London, W12 7QY

The moral right of the author has been asserted

Set in 14/20 Palatino

Made and printed in England by Clays Ltd, St Ives plc

British Library Cataloguing in Publication Data
A CIP catalogue record for this book is available from the British Library

ISBN 0–141–30452–9

Chapter One

Sheltie the Shetland pony blew a soft
snort and nuzzled Emma's outstretched
hand. He sniffed at her clenched fist,
then poked out his tongue and licked
her knuckles. Sheltie had decided that
this was the hand that held the sugar
cube. He liked this new game.

Emma grinned before she opened her
fist and held out Sheltie's prize on her
flat palm.

1

'Come on then, clever clogs! Take
your treat!' she said.

Sheltie delicately took the sugar lump
between his soft lips, then gave it a
good hard crunch.

'Sheltie's really good at that game,
isn't he?' said Sally as she rode up on
Minnow, her piebald pony. Sally was

2

Emma's best friend and Minnow was Sheltie's best pony pal.

'Minnow tries hard, but his nose isn't as keen as Sheltie's!' added Sally, patting her pony's arched neck. 'Minnow's clever all right, but I don't think there's another pony quite as clever as Sheltie.'

'Shhh!' said Emma. She quickly clamped her hands over Sheltie's ears. 'I don't want him hearing things like that and getting big-headed.'

Sheltie shook his head and blew a deafening snort.

'He could never be big-headed,' said Sally, laughing. 'And anyway, we're going to need all the brains we can get if we're going to win the "Crossways Cross-country Challenge Cup"!'

'The what?' asked Emma.

'The Crossways Cross-country Challenge Cup,' repeated Sally.

'I've never heard of it,' puzzled Emma.

'Well, you wouldn't have,' grinned Sally. 'It's new. It's the first time they've held the event. And we're going to win it!'

'How come you know all about it and I don't?' asked Emma.

'Easy-peasy,' laughed Sally. 'Daddy knows Mr and Mrs Carter who own Crossways Riding School, and they told him this morning that they've been planning this event for months. There are going to be posters all over Little Applewood and an advert in the local paper. And the prize is a big silver cup!'

'This event sounds like fun,' said Emma excitedly. 'We wouldn't want to miss it, would we, Sheltie?' The little pony tossed his head.

'And the best thing,' Sally went on, 'is that it's a team event, so we can enter together as "the Saddlebacks".'

'The Saddlebacks,' cried Emma. 'That's brilliant! The Saddlebacks ride again. We're going to win, aren't we?'

'Well, it might not be that easy,' said Sally. 'It's a cross-country event, so it's going to take a lot of stamina.'

'Well, Sheltie and I have got plenty of that,' said Emma with a laugh.

Sheltie tossed his head again and blew a long, noisy raspberry. He didn't know what Emma was saying, but he could tell that it was something exciting.

'Are there going to be entry forms and everything? And where do we get them from?'

'There are going to be trials,' said Sally. 'Next Saturday morning on the village green. If we pass the trials we can enter the competition and compete for the Crossways Cup.'

A shiver ran down Emma's spine just thinking about it. 'What will we have to do at these trials?' she asked. 'Should we be practising or something?'

'I don't know,' admitted Sally. 'All I know is that you have to pass the trials before you can enter.'

Emma held her bottom lip between her teeth and thought for a moment. 'We'd better practise everything we know,' she said. Sheltie pushed his head against Emma's arm. 'No more sugar games, boy,' Emma told him. 'You're in training!'

Chapter Two

Each day after school, Sally and
Minnow rode over to Emma's cottage to
practise for the trials. Emma and Sally
didn't know what they would have to
do, so they practised everything they
could think of.

They tried walking, trotting,
cantering, stopping on command,
turning circles and making figures of
eight. They even set up a bending

course and spent hours weaving in and out between a row of bamboo canes. Then they set up some small jumps in Sheltie's paddock and ran the circuit side by side, jumping together as a team.

'The Saddlebacks,' yelled Emma as she punched the air. 'We're going to win the cup!'

Sheltie trumpeted a loud snort and pawed at the grass.

'I wish I felt as confident as you and Sheltie,' said Sally. 'I know we're pretty good, but I've heard it's a tough course. My mum says that it's not enough just being good riders. Intelligence and stamina are really important too.'

'But Sheltie has got both of those things,' Emma protested. Sheltie bowed

his head and whickered softly.
'Intelligence and stamina. Shetland
ponies are known for it!' she said.

Sally grinned. She knew Emma was
right.

'And you and Minnow aren't *that* bad,' joked Emma cheekily.

Sally poked her tongue out. 'We're the icing on the cake,' she laughed. 'We'll just copy what you and Sheltie do and concentrate on looking good.'

Emma grinned back. It was true, Minnow looked like a top-class show pony. And Sally looked like a gymkhana queen. They were always elegant and well turned out. With Sheltie's cleverness and Minnow's style, the Saddlebacks couldn't lose!

There was just one more day before the trials and both girls were feeling excited. Posters had been pinned to trees and pasted to noticeboards advertising the event.

'I expect there will be quite a few people on the green tomorrow,' said Sally.

'Then we had better make sure we're the first ones there.' Emma reached between Sheltie's ears and gave him a good hard scratch, right on the spot where he liked it best. Sheltie closed his eyes and made a soft rumbling sound in his throat. 'You will behave, won't you, Sheltie?' she said, smiling.

On Saturday morning, Emma woke bright and early to the sound of a cockerel crowing in Mr Brown's field. She parted the bedroom curtains slightly and peered through a chink in the material.

Emma was playing a game with

Sheltie. She was trying to peep through the window without him seeing her.

But Sheltie was much better at this game than Emma. As usual, he was waiting in the paddock with his fuzzy chin resting on the top bar of the wooden fence. No matter how early Emma got up, Sheltie was always there first, watching her bedroom window.

Sheltie saw the curtains twitch and tossed back his head with a loud

whinny. Then he stamped his front feet
and wiggled his rump before setting off
on a mad dash around the paddock.
Sheltie had won again.

Emma smiled to herself as she pushed
the curtains wide open and let the
sunshine stream into the room. It was
nice waking up with a smile. And
Sheltie always made sure of that.

After a quick wash and brush-up,
Emma was on her way downstairs,
pulling up her jodhpurs as she
stumbled into the kitchen. It was all
warm and cosy downstairs and the
kitchen smelled of toast.

'Morning, Emma,' said Emma's little
brother, Joshua.

Mum was sitting with Joshua at the
kitchen table, having a cup of tea.

'You're up early, Emma,' she said.
'Couldn't you sleep?'

'It's the trials today,' said Emma
brightly.

'And the Saddlebacks are going to be
first in the queue,' teased Mum. 'There's
some toast under the grill if you've got
time.' She knew that Emma could never
resist fresh buttered toast and jam.

'Yes, please,' Emma said, plonking
herself down at the kitchen table.

Mum spread butter and jam thickly
on to Emma's toast then cut the slice
into soldiers.

'I know who would like one of these,'
Emma grinned.

'Sheltie!' yelled Joshua.

'That's right. Sheltie. And I bet he's
wondering where I've got to.' She

crammed two soldiers into her mouth then took the others out with her to the paddock.

Sheltie liked his special breakfast treat and licked the sweet jam from his lips.

'Please don't mess around at the trials, Sheltie,' whispered Emma. 'You will be good, won't you?'

The little pony tilted his head to one side and peered through his shaggy forelock with twinkling eyes. He blew a raspberry and planted a wet kiss on Emma's cheek.

'Yeuk!' she giggled. 'I take it that was a yes!'

Chapter Three

Sally and Minnow were waiting at the
stone bridge as Emma and Sheltie rode
up. Sheltie's hoofs clattered on the
cobbles as he hurried forward to meet
his pony pal.

Minnow blew a soft whicker and
nibbled at the top of Sheltie's mane.

'Are you ready, partner?' said Sally,
grinning.

'As ready as we'll ever be,' said

Emma. 'And Sheltie's promised to behave. Haven't you, boy? No pranks!'

Sheltie made as if to blow a snort, but belched instead.

'Sheltie! Manners, please!' said Emma.

Sally burst out laughing. 'The trouble with Sheltie is that you never really know what he's going to do next,' she said.

The Saddlebacks were the first riders to arrive at the green, just as they had planned. Mrs Carter was already there with an empty horsebox. The rear door was wide open and the ramp was down. Mrs Carter was busy dragging striped poles out on to the grass.

'Can we help?' asked Sally politely.

'Oh, hello, Sally,' said Mrs Carter.

'And you must be Emma?'

Sheltie blew through his lips and made a sound like a motorbike.

'That's right,' said Emma, 'and this is Sheltie. We're the Saddlebacks and we've come for the trials. I hope we'll be good enough,' she said eagerly. She leaned forward to give Sheltie's neck a pat.

'Well, why don't you help me set up these poles and then we shall see,' said Mrs Carter, smiling.

Emma and Sally slipped down from their saddles and helped Mrs Carter set up the trotting poles in a short course across the grass.

Just as they finished setting up the course, the other riders began to arrive. 'Oh, look!' said Sally. 'There's Tracy Diamond with Blaze and Alice Parker on Blue.'

Emma looked up and waved across the green at the two riders. 'And here come Robert and Dylan with Toffee and Sabre,' she added. More and more riders began to arrive.

Mrs Carter called everyone to attention and asked the riders to stand in pairs.

Then she spoke to each team and took down their names and details. Emma and Sally were first.

'You're the Saddlebacks, right?' Mrs Carter said, smiling. 'Now give me your full names.'

'Emma Matthews and Sally Jones,' said Emma, as the butterflies danced in her stomach.

When everyone's names had been taken, the trials began. Emma and Sally went first.

'I want you to canter Sheltie and Minnow to the end of the green,' announced Mrs Carter. 'Ride as a pair

and keep together, side by side. Then
turn at the oak tree, circling the trunk
twice, and trot back over the cavaletti
poles.'

'Easy-peasy,' whispered Emma. She
gave Sally a high five, slapping palms
with her partner.

Chapter Four

Sheltie and Minnow took the course easily. Minnow's long, elegant strides seemed effortless, and Sheltie's little fat legs pumped away to keep up. Despite their difference in size, Sheltie and Minnow were a perfect pair.

When everyone had taken a turn and Mrs Carter had made some notes on her clipboard, she used the cavaletti poles to set up three small jumps.

The first jump was very low. The
second was about seven bricks high.
And the third jump was over two
crossed poles. *That* jump looked higher
than it really was. The trick was to jump
at the lowest point where the poles
crossed in the middle.

Again, the Saddlebacks went first.
Emma and Sally couldn't ride side
by side this time, but they still had to
stay close together, one behind the
other.

Sheltie loved jumping. And although
he was small, he looked just like a
showjumping champion.

Sheltie tossed his head as he
approached the first jump and cleared it
easily. He didn't really need to jump so
high. Sheltie was just showing off in

24

front of the crowd. He soared over the second jump and took the crossed poles perfectly in the centre.

Minnow followed closely behind. Sally was an excellent rider and her pony was used to jumping, but somehow Minnow clipped the crossed poles with his hind hoof.

'He should have cleared that easily,' said Sally. 'Minnow doesn't usually drop a hoof.'

Sally was worried that Minnow's mistake might stop the Saddlebacks from entering the competition, but their second round was perfect.

The last test was cantering three times around the green non-stop, with a full gallop down the final length.

Mr Thorne, the vet, gave each pony a

quick check-up when they'd finished their gallop.

'All ponies have to be fighting fit for a cross-country event,' he told the riders.

Examining Sheltie was normally quite easy for Mr Thorne. But this time there were lots of other ponies around and Sheltie was starting to get frisky.

Each time Mr Thorne tried to place his stethoscope on Sheltie's chest, the little pony grabbed the end in his mouth and pulled it away from the vet.

'Now, come on, Sheltie,' said Mr Thorne. 'Be a good boy and let me do my job!' He tried again. But Sheltie was too full of mischief.

'Sheltie!' warned Emma. She used her best 'no nonsense' voice and Sheltie's ears twitched. At last he stood still.

'Sheltie's as fit as a fiddle, the little
rascal,' Mr Thorne laughed. Then, as if
Sheltie had heard, he nudged the vet
playfully on the bottom as he turned to
examine Minnow.

Every pony at the green that day
passed both the trials and the fitness

test. All that was left was for Mrs Carter to tell everyone about the Crossways Cross-country Challenge and what they would have to do on the day of the competition.

'It's a six-mile course,' she announced. 'But from what I've seen today, I don't think there will be anyone here who won't be able to complete the route.'

Emma put up her hand. 'Sally's mum says that it takes dedicated riders and intelligent ponies to complete a cross-country event,' she said.

Mrs Carter smiled. 'That's true,' she said. 'But I'm sure you'll all be fine.' Then she went on to explain the rules and the layout of the course.

When Mrs Carter had finished,

everyone collected a map showing the
six-mile route through the countryside.

'Although the course is clearly
marked,' said Mrs Carter, 'the jumps
and obstacles are not shown. That will
make the competition extra special
because there will be lots of surprises on
the day.' She smiled.

Emma showed Sheltie the map. She
held it in front of his face and explained,
'This is the course, Sheltie. Six long
miles, with jumps and obstacles, and a
silver cup at the end!'

Sheltie harrumphed, then blew a
noisy raspberry and licked the map.

'I don't think Sheltie's bothered about
the cup,' said Sally.

'He just likes having fun,' grinned
Emma. 'But you'll do your best, won't

you, boy?' Sheltie bobbed his head and made his long shaggy forelock fall across his face.

'Perhaps tomorrow we can ride round the course and see what it's like,' suggested Sally.

'That's a good idea,' said Emma. 'A kind of dress rehearsal!'

Sheltie jangled his reins and tossed his head up and down.

Emma ruffled Sheltie's mane. 'You think that's a good idea too, don't you, boy?'

Chapter Five

As Emma went to fetch Sheltie from the paddock on Sunday morning, she held the map of the course in her hand. She waved it in front of him. 'We're going to win that silver cup next week,' she told him.

Sheltie wrinkled his nose and blew a lively snort. Then he tried to snaffle the piece of paper. The little Shetland pony was raring to go. Emma could tell he was really looking forward to the cross-country challenge.

Emma had arranged to meet Sally at the village green, which was where the cross-country ride was going to start.

When she arrived at the green, Emma found Sally and Minnow waiting

patiently beneath the big oak tree. Sally
had been studying her copy of the route
as well.

'I don't recognize any of these paths,'
she said. 'I'm sure I've never ridden on
any of them before.'

'Yes, you have,' said Emma. 'We've
been down some of these bridle paths
together. You just can't remember!'

'It's all right for you,' said Sally with
a smile. 'You and Sheltie know Little
Applewood like the back of your hand.
Or hoof,' she added with a laugh.

'But we're a team,' said Emma. 'We're
the Saddlebacks, remember? So it
doesn't matter. We're going to stick
together. It's in the rules. We must never
be further than five metres apart. And
there will be marshals at the jumps to

make sure we stick to the course, so we can't get lost!'

Suddenly Sally felt silly for worrying. But she couldn't help it. She wasn't as adventurous as Emma. And although Minnow was a fantastic pony, he wasn't as brave as Sheltie. Minnow got nervous in unfamiliar territory, but Sheltie thought every new turn and bridle path was an adventure.

'Right,' announced Emma. 'Let's try out the course. I'll lead the way on Sheltie. It'll be great!'

They set off, following the route on the map. First they went round Barrow Hill, then they entered the woods. The path through the trees would lead them in a wide arc around the edge of the downs and into the Molland Valley.

Sheltie trotted ahead, rustling his way through the fresh fall of autumn leaves. The sky overhead was not so bright now, and dark clouds were rolling in from the moor. It felt a bit chilly in the shadow of the woods, and the two girls pulled up their collars.

Suddenly the trees thinned out and they could see the Molland Valley in front of them.

'I don't think I've ever ridden here before,' said Sally.

Sheltie flared his nostrils and took in the scent of the valley with a deep breath.

'Yes, you have,' Emma told Sally. 'The main road runs over that rise, remember? It's beautiful, isn't it?'

Sally smiled. She wasn't so sure. A

shiver had suddenly run down her spine.

'What's the matter, Sally?' asked Emma. 'What's wrong?'

'Nothing,' lied Sally.

'Yes, there is,' said Emma. 'I can tell!'

'Well,' Sally began, 'it's just that I've heard stories about this valley being haunted.' She grinned sheepishly and felt a bit silly. 'You don't think we're going to run into any ghosts, do you?'

Emma smiled. And Sheltie seemed to smile too, by curling back his lips. Then he blew a series of high whinnies that echoed through the valley.

'I've heard stories like that too,' Emma told her. 'But Mum and Dad say that's all they are. Just stories.'

'I hope your mum and dad are right,' said Sally. She studied the map. 'This route takes us right through the centre of the valley,' she said. 'Then it crosses that stream and disappears into the forest on the other side.'

'Now that's one place we've never been to, isn't it, Sheltie?' said Emma. 'The forest!'

Sheltie blew a noisy snort and looked

up at the sky. His keen nose could smell rain in the air.

'Come on then,' urged Sally. 'The sooner we complete this course, the sooner we can start planning the best way to tackle it on the day.'

'And win the cup,' grinned Emma.

Sally squeezed with her legs and urged Minnow forward.

'Trot on,' said Emma. 'And don't step on any ghosts, Sheltie!' she teased.

Sally laughed and poked Emma in the ribs.

Chapter Six

Halfway through the valley, Emma suggested they try a jump. Up ahead she had spotted a fallen log. It lay across the bridle path and was perfect for a practice leap.

'I'll go first,' announced Emma. She took Sheltie up to the log at a fast gallop. His little legs were moving so quickly that all Sally could see was a blur. Then Sheltie took off and cleared the log by half a metre.

'Yippee!' Emma yelled as they landed in a pile of leaves. 'Come on, Sally. Your turn!'

Sally rode Minnow at a canter and approached the jump with an easy stride. Then they took off. It was a simple jump for Minnow and he should have sailed over with plenty of room to spare. But he dropped a hind leg and thumped the log with his hoof.

When he landed, Minnow started to limp. And to make matters worse, it started to rain.

'Oh, no,' moaned Sally. 'That's all we need.'

'Come on. Let's take shelter in the forest,' suggested Emma.

Sheltie took the lead and trotted over

towards the cover of a thick line of trees. Emma let him choose the way while Minnow limped along behind. Sally didn't think that Minnow was lame, but *something* was wrong. Every third step he raised his hoof and hobbled for a few paces.

Sheltie soon discovered a muddy track and, before Emma could stop him, the little pony was halfway down it.

Up ahead, they could see a small stone cottage. It was an old, tumbledown building with ivy growing up its walls and over the roof. Some of the glass in the windows was cracked and patched up with tape, and there were weeds growing in the cracks in the stone walls.

'It looks haunted,' whispered Sally.

'I'm sure it is. It looks so dark and
spooky.'

'Don't be silly,' said Emma. 'It's just
empty!'

'Empty *and* haunted,' argued Sally.

Then Emma saw the covered log store
next to the building. 'Well, it's a perfect

place to take shelter,' she said. 'Haunted or not!'

As she spoke, lightning flashed through the clouds and the dark sky rumbled.

'Come on, then,' said Sally.

They huddled with their ponies beneath the tin roof of the log store and listened to the rain pelting the thin tin above them. Sheltie shook out his soggy mane and sprayed water over everyone.

'I hope the rain stops soon,' said Sally. 'I'm worried about Minnow's leg. I want to get back and let someone look at it.'

'It's probably just a stone in his hoof,' said Emma. 'Shall we have a look?'

The rain slowed to a drizzle and a cold draught blew through the shelter.

Sally shivered. 'Thanks,' she said. 'But I just want to get away from here. Let's look at Minnow's hoof later. This place gives me the creeps.'

Just then, the front door of the cottage flew open. Emma and Sally gasped in fright as the pale, ghostly figure of an elderly man appeared. Sally stifled a scream.

Emma tried to speak, but her voice only came out as a whispered croak. Perhaps this *was* a haunted cottage after all!

It was Sheltie who made the first move. The little pony jangled his bit, then poked out his tongue and blew a raspberry before nuzzling the man's pale, ghostly hand.

The ghostly old man smiled. His face

didn't look so spooky when he grinned.
Then he spoke, and the two girls
realized that he wasn't a ghost at all.

'Hello. I'm Mr Maguire,' he said.
Then he stroked Sheltie's nose and
ruffled the pony's damp forelock. 'What
a nice friendly chappie!'

Sheltie whickered softly and raised
his hoof in greeting.

'Well, look at that,' said Mr Maguire,

smiling. 'He's a real charmer, isn't he?'

Emma and Sally exchanged looks. They both felt a bit embarrassed for thinking that Mr Maguire was a ghost. Here they were, taking shelter on his property, and they hadn't even said hello.

Emma spoke up. 'I hope you didn't mind us sheltering here,' she said. 'Only it was pouring with rain and we didn't think anyone lived here. Sheltie led us along the track to your cottage.'

'He's a very clever pony then,' Mr Maguire told them. 'Not many people can find my cottage. And that's how I like it,' he added.

'We're really sorry for disturbing you,' said Emma, feeling worried. Mr Maguire just smiled.

'We thought you were a ghost,' said Sally. She hadn't meant to say it, but she was nervous and it just slipped out. Emma nudged her in the ribs. 'Ouch!' she squealed.

'It's all right,' said Mr Maguire, with a smile. He didn't look so old and spooky now. 'I'm used to people thinking things like that. There are lots of silly stories about the valley being haunted, and lots of them are about me and my ramshackle cottage.'

Emma giggled loudly. She had just noticed the sign that said 'Ramshackle Cottage' nailed next to the front door.

Chapter Seven

Mr Maguire didn't normally like visitors, but he seemed happy to chat away with Emma and Sally. He told them that he didn't like electricity, telephones or television either.

'In fact, I don't like modern ways at all,' he said. 'I cook on an old range and light the cottage with candles.' Mr Maguire was an old-fashioned man.

'I don't often see folk from Little Applewood or the other villages,' he explained. 'I usually prefer to keep myself to myself.' He stroked Sheltie's shaggy mane as he spoke. 'You're the first visitors I've had since the summer,' he said. 'I hope I didn't frighten you too much.'

Emma and Sally smiled. Mr Maguire was strange and funny-looking, with his thin face and shock of white hair, but he was a kind man and he obviously loved animals.

'We're practising for a competition,' said Emma. 'A cross-country event,' she added. 'Only Minnow here keeps dropping a hoof when he jumps and we think he's going lame.'

'Oh dear,' sighed Mr Maguire.

Sally smiled shyly. She wasn't as good at explaining as Emma.

'I could have a look at that hoof if you like,' offered Mr Maguire. 'I'm good with ponies.' Sheltie sniffed at his new friend's clothes and nibbled at Mr Maguire's tatty cardigan with his teeth. It smelt of peppermints.

'Stop that, Sheltie,' scolded Emma. 'Don't forget your manners!'

'It's all right,' said Mr Maguire, laughing. 'I've got plenty of moth holes already, so one more hole won't make any difference. Now let me look at this hoof.'

Minnow raised his leg and let Mr Maguire examine his shoe.

'Mmm. Just as I thought,' he said. 'It's not a stone at all. It's a loose nail. Part of it has broken off and caught under the shoe. It probably hurts when he puts his full weight on it just before a jump.'

'Poor Minnow,' said Sally. 'Will it be all right to ride him home?' The rain

had almost stopped, but the forest was still dripping all around them.

'I think it's best to take the nail right out,' said Mr Maguire. 'Just to be on the safe side. I can do that for you quite easily. And put in a new one. I used to keep ponies here in the forest.' He smiled. 'Now, how about a nice hot drink to sip while I fix Minnow's shoe? Hot blackcurrant juice. I make it myself in the press. You can't get fresher! I'll go and make some now.'

Minutes later, Mr Maguire came out of Ramshackle Cottage with two steaming mugs for Emma and Sally and a few sugar lumps for Sheltie and Minnow.

'Don't just give them to him,' said Emma. 'Make Sheltie earn them.' She showed Mr Maguire Sheltie's new trick. She held out two clenched hands so that Sheltie had to choose the one hiding the sugar.

'He's very good at that, isn't he?' said their new friend, smiling.

'Minnow's not though,' sighed Sally. 'He's not interested in that game.'

'Oh, but I bet he likes doing other things,' said Mr Maguire. 'I bet he can race like the wind and jump like a grasshopper.'

'He can jump higher than a grasshopper,' laughed Sally.

'Well, now that's something, isn't it?' said the old man. 'It's higher than I can manage!'

Emma and Sally both laughed. They liked Mr Maguire. He looked strange and he had some old-fashioned ways, but he was so nice and kind.

Sheltie liked Mr Maguire too. After he had finished all the sugar lumps, Sheltie started to nuzzle Mr Maguire's big, baggy, peppermint cardigan.

'Come on, Sheltie,' said Emma. 'Leave Mr Maguire alone and let him see to Minnow.'

Sheltie shook his reins, snorted and stepped back while Mr Maguire fixed Minnow's shoe.

Some time later, Sheltie whickered goodbye, and the two girls led their ponies back up the track and out into the valley.

'Come and see me again, if you like,' Mr Maguire called after them. 'I don't usually like visitors. But you're

welcome. Visit any time.' Then he
shuffled back inside the cottage and
closed the door.

'Bye, Mr Maguire,' called Emma.

'Thanks for fixing Minnow's shoe,'
Sally added.

But Mr Maguire had already gone.

Chapter Eight

A week later, Emma and Sally were in Sheltie's paddock having one last practice before the Crossways Cross-country Challenge.

'I think we should practise jumping crossed poles,' said Emma. 'I bet there'll be crossed poles on the course,' she added. 'After all, Mrs Carter set up crossed poles at the trials, didn't she?'

Sheltie looked up and snorted.

'I hope so,' said Sally. 'Minnow loves jumping, don't you, boy?' She patted her pony's neck. 'Come on, then, where are those crossed poles?'

On the day of the Crossways Cross-country Challenge, Emma and Sally were surprised to see so many teams taking part. The green was filled with ponies of all shapes and sizes.

There were stocky little rough ponies, sleek show ponies, shaggy hill ponies, and lots of ponies from local stables. Mrs Carter had been holding trials in the other nearby villages too. But there was only one Shetland pony competing.

Sheltie's eyes were twinkling with excitement. He had never seen so many

ponies in one place before. He sniffed
the air and neighed very loudly. All the
other ponies glanced across. Some
looked away again, but most answered
with soft snorts and grunts. It was the
ponies' way of saying hello.

Emma counted at least thirty ponies. 'That means fifteen pairs,' she exclaimed.

'It's a good job we're all being timed separately,' said Sally.

'We'd never be able to ride out together. And it will be easier to follow the markers round the course in pairs,' added Emma.

Just then, Mrs Carter came over and handed Emma and Sally two squares with numbers on them to pin on each other's back.

'We're number thirteen,' exclaimed Emma. 'That's lucky, isn't it?'

'Lucky for some,' Sally answered. She wasn't so sure. She had always thought that number thirteen was *unlucky*.

They pinned on their numbers and took their places in line behind the starting post. A marshal was making notes of the time as each pair galloped away.

'There will be more marshals along the course,' whispered Emma. 'Every time there's a jump or an obstacle, a marshal will be there to watch.'

'That's to make sure no one cheats,' added Sally cleverly.

'And to give marks,' Emma reminded her.

Suddenly, their number was announced. 'Team number thirteen,' called the marshal. 'Emma Matthews and Sally Jones riding as the Saddlebacks. Take your positions.'

Emma tightened her reins. 'Here goes,

boy,' she whispered. Then she squeezed
Sheltie's fat sides with her legs. 'Go,
Sheltie. Go!'

Chapter Nine

Emma cantered Sheltie out of the village and up towards Barrow Hill, with Sally and Minnow following close behind. They followed the green ribbon markers and rode towards the woods on the rise of the downs.

'Easy-peasy, so far,' called Emma. Sheltie was really enjoying himself and trotted along with a springy bounce.

Up ahead, at the edge of the wood,

Emma spotted a marshal. 'Here comes the first jump,' she called. And she was right. It was a low jump made from bales of hay.

Sheltie was really showing off in front of the marshal and jumped far too high. But he looked spectacular. Sally took Minnow over at an easy stride and gave Emma the thumbs-up.

The ride through the woods took them through an obstacle course of bending poles. There were eight canes set in a line, two metres apart. Sheltie and Minnow had to weave in and out of the canes without touching any of them.

Sheltie was normally very good at this. Emma hoped that he would be brilliant today and not pull any of the canes out with his teeth. Weaving in and out was easy. Getting Sheltie to behave was the tricky bit.

'Yes!' cried Emma as Sheltie trotted round the last cane. She glanced over her shoulder and smiled at the marshal. Sally and Minnow completed the course perfectly too.

The Saddlebacks rode on. Ahead of them lay the Molland Valley. They had followed the markers down to the stream and were crossing over a line of stepping stones.

'Isn't this fantastic!' cried Emma. 'Just riding out here today is brilliant. And won't it be great if we win the cup?'

Just then, as if Sheltie had heard what Emma had said, he suddenly put on a spurt and hurried along the bridle path. But then he surprised Emma by veering off towards a line of trees.

Sally and Minnow followed, as Emma tried to pull Sheltie up and rein him in. But the little pony was determined to take them into the wood. He tossed up his head and sniffed the air. Sheltie could smell something.

'What's going on?' asked Sally. 'Where's Sheltie taking us?' She looked around, then suddenly recognized her surroundings.

'I think this track will take us to Mr Maguire's cottage again,' announced Emma.

'I think you're right,' said Sally.

'Sorry, Sally,' Emma sighed. 'Sheltie is wasting valuable time. But he's so determined, I can't stop him. I don't know what's the matter with him.'

As they turned a bend in the track, Emma could see Mr Maguire's cottage, which lay at the end of the muddy path. She quickly realized something was wrong. Something was *terribly* wrong.

Thick smoke was billowing from the chimney of Ramshackle Cottage.

Emma urged Sheltie to gallop on. Sally and Minnow were right behind them, and within seconds they were all peering through Mr Maguire's window.

Sheltie's breath steamed up the glass, and Emma had to wipe the window to see properly. It was dark inside and the room was full of smoke. Emma cupped her hands round her eyes for a better look. Then she gasped in horror as she saw Mr Maguire lying on the floor inside.

A big fire was roaring in the hearth, and a burning log had rolled out on to the floor. Not only was the chimney on fire, but smoke and flames were about

to burn their way across the bare
floorboards.

'He must have fallen,' cried Emma.
'He must have fallen and knocked
himself out!'

She rapped on the window, just in

case Mr Maguire was awake and could hear her.

He didn't move.

Sally dropped Minnow's reins and ran to the front door. She rattled the handle, but the door was locked. 'What are we going to do?' she cried. 'Mr Maguire's trapped inside.'

'We could get Sheltie and Minnow to kick down the door,' said Emma. 'But smashing windows and opening doors can sometimes make a fire worse. And we couldn't move him by ourselves.'

Sheltie was snorting excitedly and pawing at the ground. The little pony could smell the smoke and seemed to know that Mr Maguire was trapped inside.

Sally started to panic. 'We've got to

do something.' Her voice sounded shaky. Minnow was upset too. He was edgy and pulled at his reins to get away from the smoke.

Emma didn't have much time to think. Something had to be done quickly.

Minnow was a much bigger pony and a lot faster than little Sheltie. He would have been able to cover the distance back to the village in next to no time. But Emma knew that Minnow was nervous in strange countryside and the going was quite rough. And Sally didn't know the area as well as Emma.

There was only one thing to do. Emma and Sally decided that Sally should stay at the cottage while Emma took Sheltie and went for help.

'I could ride back and try to find a marshal,' said Emma. 'But we were almost the last through and they've probably gone back to the village.'

'Anyway, what could a marshal do?' said Sally. 'What we really need is the fire brigade. If you go and call them, Minnow and I can keep a lookout from the top of the rise. When they get here, we can show the firemen where the cottage is.'

'That's a great idea,' Emma agreed. 'There's a telephone box at the foot of Barrow Hill,' she told Sally. 'Sheltie and I can cut across country and be there in less than ten minutes.'

'Can't you just go back the way we came?' worried Sally. 'It'll be much safer.'

'It would take too long,' Emma replied. 'We just don't have time.' She turned Sheltie away from the burning cottage and swung herself up into the saddle. 'You can do it, can't you, boy?'

Sheltie made several gruff snorts and chewed on his bit. The little pony was ready for anything. Sheltie was small, but he was sturdy and strong and full of stamina.

Emma kicked him on and Sheltie took off with a great burst of speed.

Chapter Ten

Sheltie's hoofs drummed the ground with an urgent beat as he flew back up the track. Emma glanced quickly over her shoulder and gasped as fresh flames roared from the chimney. 'Come on, boy,' she urged. 'Every second counts.'

The little pony was going as fast as he knew how. Trees and bushes flashed past as Sheltie and Emma tore through the forest and out into the valley.

Their first obstacle was the stream. Emma didn't have time to ride Sheltie back to the stepping stones they had crossed on the way. They would have to jump straight over.

The stream wasn't deep, but it was quite wide. Sheltie had cleared much wider obstacles before, but Emma was worried about the ground on the other bank. It was rough and muddy, and she didn't want him to slip.

Sheltie's pace didn't slow or falter and they rode the stream at a thundering pace. Sheltie soared across and landed on solid ground on the far bank. It was a perfect jump. 'Well done, boy,' Emma cried as she clapped Sheltie's neck. Then they were away again, galloping through the valley.

A cold wind whipped through Sheltie's mane as he settled into his stride. It was difficult riding on such rough ground, but Sheltie didn't falter.

Soon they came to another obstacle. There was a low hedge of gorse blocking their path. It was quite high, but the little pony took off with a tremendous leap and sailed clean over.

They were past the woods now and almost out of the valley. The telephone box was only minutes away.

But when they reached it, Emma's heart sank. There was a notice plastered across the door which said 'SORRY, OUT OF ORDER'.

'Oh, no!' cried Emma. 'What now?'

Then she thought of the fire station in Little Applewood. It was only a small station and was run by volunteers, so it was not always manned. Emma hoped someone would be there. She knew she was running out of time.

The countryside sloped down towards the village. There was only one ditch and one fence to cross now, and then they would be back in Little Applewood. But the ditch was easy to

stumble into by accident if you didn't know it was there. It was difficult to see in the boggy field in front of them.

Emma pulled Sheltie up to take the ditch carefully. If they misjudged this one, then Sheltie would be in real trouble.

With a sudden burst of speed, Sheltie leapt forward with every bit of his strength. The dark ditch disappeared beneath them as they sailed across.

But something terrible happened. Sheltie had cleared the ditch easily enough, but he landed very badly. He struggled to keep his footing. Emma did everything she could, but Sheltie stumbled and fell.

Emma was frightened that Sheltie might be badly hurt, but somehow he

managed to scramble up with Emma
still in the saddle. Everything happened
so quickly that the accident hardly
broke their stride.

Emma slowed Sheltie down to a
gentle canter. She didn't want to risk
another accident. They were almost

there. There was just one last fence between them and help for Mr Maguire.

As they approached the fence, Emma saw that there was a broken five-bar gate to one side. The fence was high, but the top two bars of the gate were hanging down and crossed at a lower height. It was just like the crossed poles that Mrs Carter had set up at the trials.

The run up to the gate was straight and clean. Emma knew that Sheltie could do it. He was the best pony in the world. It was now or never.

Chapter Eleven

Sheltie took off and soared like a bird.
He flew higher and higher, as though he
were heading for the clouds.

'Yes! Well done, Sheltie!' cried Emma.
They had done it. Sheltie raced across
the field towards the village and the fire
station.

Emma rode Sheltie up to the station,
then slipped from the saddle and ran
with him up to the big double doors.

Sheltie was puffing and blowing after his cross-country race. The big doors were slightly ajar and Emma peered inside.

'Oh, no,' she cried. The fire engine had gone. The station was empty!

Sheltie blew a loud snort. He seemed as disappointed as Emma.

Then suddenly, a side door swung open and in walked John Bishop, a volunteer firefighter from the village. Emma had never been so glad to see anyone in her life.

She quickly blurted out her story and Mr Bishop sped into action. He had been outside checking over the fire engine in the back yard with another volunteer. The small, modern engine was there and ready to go!

'I'll follow on Sheltie,' yelled Emma
as the fireman pulled on his coat and
ran off around the back.

Emma leapt into the saddle. 'Come
on, boy!' she said. 'Are you ready for
one more ride?' The little pony
answered with a lively snort. Emma
patted Sheltie's sweating neck. Sheltie's

ears twitched. He was ready for anything!

They galloped forward, chasing the fire engine as it sped off on its rescue mission.

The ride back seemed to take less time. But now Sheltie knew what to expect. He took the ditch and all the jumps like a true champion.

As they crossed the valley and raced through the woods, Emma and Sheltie could hear the fire siren sounding. It was coming from over the rise on the road behind Mr Maguire's cottage.

Emma knew Sally and Minnow would be waiting to show the firemen the way. She just hoped they would get there in time!

As Emma and Sheltie raced up the

track, they could see that smoke was still pouring from the chimney pot. But John Bishop was already in action, unwinding the big hose.

'Over here,' called Sally. Sheltie whickered as if he was surprised. Neither Sheltie nor Emma was expecting to see Mr Maguire sitting with Sally on a bench, a little way from the cottage.

'Mr Maguire woke up after you left,' said Sally. 'But he couldn't open the door, so I got Minnow to kick it down. Mr Maguire managed to crawl out of the cottage just in time, before the ceiling collapsed.'

The old man sat with his head in his hands as the fire was brought under control.

'What will you do?' asked Emma. Mr Maguire couldn't possibly live in Ramshackle Cottage now. It was more of a ruin than ever.

'I suppose I've got to wake up to the modern world after all,' he said. 'I've got a sister in Eastbourne who's always

nagging me to go and live with her. I think I'll go and give her a surprise!'

Emma and Sally looked at each other and smiled.

'But what about your contest?' he asked.

Emma and Sally had forgotten all about the Crossways Cross-country Challenge.

'It'll all be over by now,' said Sally. 'They'll be announcing the winners soon.'

'And awarding the cup,' added Emma.

'Shall we ride back to Little Applewood and watch the presentation?' Sally suggested.

Emma nodded. 'Come on then!' she said.

When the Saddlebacks rode on to the village green, a huge cheer rang out. Sheltie held his head high and tossed his mane. Emma and Sally exchanged glances and giggled. Minnow flicked up his ears and blew a snort.

John Bishop had reported the fire to the police, and PC McDonald had told Mrs Carter about the Saddlebacks' brave rescue.

'Although Emma and Sally didn't complete the course with their ponies, Sheltie and Minnow,' announced Mrs Carter, 'it gives me great pleasure to award these special rosettes for outstanding bravery to the Saddlebacks.'

Everyone cheered again as Mrs Carter

pinned a big blue rosette on to Sheltie's
bridle and another on to Minnow's.
Sheltie held up his head and looked
very proud.

Emma leaned across to Sally and took
her friend's hand. 'Three cheers for the
Saddlebacks!' she cried. And Sheltie and
Minnow joined in with their loudest
whinnies.

Another **Sheltie** *book available in Puffin*

Sheltie

The Big Surprise

The little pony with the big heart!

It's spring at last! Emma and Sheltie can't wait
to go out and about and make new friends.
But there's trouble up on the moors. A ewe is
desperately ill, a nosy lamb wanders too far
from the flock and, back in the village, there's
chaos when a travelling magician's rabbits
escape.

If you like making friends, fun, excitement
and adventure, then you'll love

The little pony with the big heart!

Sheltie is the lovable little Shetland pony with a big
personality. He is cheeky, full of fun and has a heart
of gold. His owner, Emma, knew that she and Sheltie
would be best friends as soon as she saw him. She
could tell that he thought so too by the way his
brown eyes twinkled beneath his big, bushy mane.
When Emma, her mum and dad and little brother,
Joshua, first moved to Little Applewood, she thought
that she might not like living there. But life is
never dull with Sheltie around. He is full of
mischief and he and Emma have lots of exciting
adventures together.

Share Sheltie and Emma's adventures in:

SHELTIE THE SHETLAND PONY
SHELTIE SAVES THE DAY
SHELTIE AND THE RUNAWAY
SHELTIE FINDS A FRIEND
SHELTIE TO THE RESCUE
SHELTIE IN DANGER